FOXY TALES

Caryl Hart AND Alex T. Smith

ALPHONSO

FOXY

A DIVISION O

Text copyright © 2015 Caryl Hart
Illustrations copyright © 2015 Alex T. Smith

First published in Great Britain in 2015 by Hodder Children's Books

The right of Caryl Hart to be identified as the author and
Alex T. Smith to be identified as the illustrator of this Work has
been asserted by them in accordance with the Copyright, Designs
and Patents Act 1988.

FIRST EDITION

10 9 8 7 6 5 4 3 2 1

Design by Alison Still

A catalogue record for this book is available from the British Library

978 1 444 90933 3
Printed and bound by CPI Group (UK) Ltd, Croydon, CR0 4YY

The paper and board used in this paperback by Hodder Children's
Books are natural recyclable products made from wood grown in
sustainable forests. The manufacturing processes conform to the
environmental regulations of the country of origin.

Hodder Children's Books
a division of Hachette Children's Books
338 Euston Road, London NW1 3BH
www.hachette.co.uk

Foxy DuBois and

Alphonso Alligator

in:

The Great Jail Break

In which Foxy and Alphonso find themselves in a very tight place. Can they escape? Or will it be a life behind bars for these two hapless rogues?

Introducing
Foxy DuBois

She's smart. She's cute.
And she'll do anything
to get rid of Alphonso.

and
Alphonso the Alligator

He's mean.
He's hungry.
And if Foxy doesn't
feed him he's going
to eat HER!

and Tony Ravioli

He's... err... he's the barman.

and Special Guest

Mr Billy Bongo
as Eric-the-Evil

Yep, he's cute... err...
I mean... dastardly.

WARNING:

Contains scenes of frilly knickers
and a large tickly feather, which
some readers may find distressing.

DISCLAIMER:

No animals were humiliated, teased or
eaten in the production of this book.

*F*oxy Dubois is really very well-bred and from a long line of very wealthy foxes. But now her life is in ruins, thanks to one rather large, rather loud and ill-mannered alligator. Alphonso first rolled up to Foxy's grand front door many moons ago, when he was just an egg. A HUUUUUGE egg, but an egg none-the-less. Since that fateful day he has done nothing but annoy and intimidate poor Foxy. It's not surprising she is desperate to get rid of him. If only she could work out how...

Of course, Alphonso isn't deliberately bad. Yes, he smells. Yes, he is rude and has terrible table manners, but Alphonso Alligator was not born bad. But he IS badly behaved. And he doesn't care about Foxy DuBois because once, a long long time ago – when he was a poor defenceless egg – that scheming fox threatened to eat him. And for this he has never, ever forgiven her. So now Alphonso treats Foxy DuBois as a meal-ticket-on-legs. And if she doesn't keep him fed, he could always eat HER.

Welcome to Vaudeville. It's getting dark. And it's quiet. Too quiet. Do you feel at home? Do you feel safe?

Well, if I were you I'd skedaddle off to your cosy little house and bolt the door. Double bolt it if you can, because these streets are filled with shady characters and unsavoury fiends.

Hear that? It's a police siren. Watch out! It's coming this way!

'It's the Vaudeville City Bank!'
a police officer shouts. 'There's
been a robbery!'

You turn just in time to see two
shadowy figures, one large, one
small. They emerge from a
darkened doorway and make off
down the street carrying a large
sack. Are they giggling? It's hard
to tell. But you can be sure as eggs
is eggs that they are up to no good.

Chapter 1

In which Foxy and Alphonso have rather a lot of money

'We've got mon-ee! We've got mon-ee! We've got mon-ee and so we are happee!' Standing in the doorway of the East Street Eazy Diner, arm in arm, were a hideously ugly alligator with VERY sharp teeth, and a small, smartly-dressed fox.

The owner of the diner, one Tony Ravioli, grabbed a pair of oven gloves and clamped them tightly around his head. His customers dived for cover, and crouched, trembling under their tables.

'The singing!'

they groaned.

'Make it stop!'

But Alphonso the alligator and Foxy DuBois didn't stop. They were swaying and staggering under the weight of a huge brown sack and smiling all over their faces.

'Hey, Tony!' grinned Alphonso. 'Look what WE got!' He heaved the sack onto a table and emptied out its contents. 'Give me three of EVERYTHING on the menu!' he beamed. 'And the same for the fox.'

Tony Ravioli stared in disbelief
at the enormous pile of
twinkling gold coins. 'What
the...? Where the heck did you
get that lot from?' he gasped.

'We... err... found it,' said Foxy.

'You found it?' said Tony.

'Yeah,' said Alphonso. 'I was peckish, so we went into town for a midnight snack.

I was just about to climb in the back window of the bakery, when two men in fancy dress ran out of the bank next door and tripped over my tail.'

'And when they saw Alphonso's teeth,' said Foxy, 'they just sort of dropped this sack and ran off.'

Elbowing Foxy out of the way, Alphonso added, 'So we took it before they could ask for it back... Owwwww!'

Foxy kicked Alphonso in the shins. 'You promised not to tell anyone that bit!' she hissed. 'I should have known not to trust you.'

'Well it WAS a bit dim of you,' Alphonso smirked.

'Why, you ungrateful, ugly orangutan!' said Foxy. 'I'll have you know I'm the smartest fox in this whole darned city. I was rich and happy and popular before you came along and ruined everything. Why, oh why did you have to turn up at my door? I had a life. I had fun. I had crockery!'

'You just can't stand the fact that I'm bigger and stronger and more intelligent that you!' growled Alphonso.

24

'No you're not!'
shrieked Foxy.

'Yes I am!'
yelled Alphonso.

'Are not!'

'SHUDDUP OR I'LL EAT YOU!'

The pair launched themselves at each other, punching and kicking and yelling until a police officer strode into the East Street Eazy Diner and pulled them apart.

'Stop right where you are, you felons,' she shouted. 'I am arresting you on suspicion of pinching a lot of money that isn't yours. You are to accompany me to my vehicle. Then I will convey you, without delay, to a secure establishment where you will be tried in a court of law.'

'Is she talking to us?' hissed Alphonso. Foxy shrugged.

The police officer sighed, grabbed Foxy and Alphonso by the scruffs of their necks and marched them out of the diner. 'Just get in the van!' she snapped.

Chapter 2

In which Foxy and Alphonso encounter the Feather of Doom

'I hereby sentence you both to six months in a secure correction unit,' boomed the judge. 'Do you have anything to say for yourselves?'

'Do they have nice food?' asked Alphonso. 'I'm starving!'

Foxy leapt to her feet. 'This is an outrage!' she shouted. 'Anyone can see that I'm innocent!' But her shouts were met with stony silence. She tried again. 'But Alphonso made me do it,' she pleaded. 'Besides, I was desperate to get away from that hideous lizard and back to the high life I deserve. You can't blame me for keeping just a few little coins to buy some modestly-priced shoes and a teensy-weensy little train ticket. What if I say sorry and promise not to do it again? Surely you'll let me off?'

'Not a chance,' said the judge.
'Court dismissed!'

Four burly officers hauled Foxy
DuBois and Alphonso Alligator
away.

'I can't believe my life has come to
this!' wailed Foxy. 'I don't belong
in jail! I'm nice!'

'No you're not,' snapped Alphonso.

'Yes I am...'

'Welcome to The Vaudeville Correction Unit,' shouted a man in uniform. 'My name is Warden Gordon. Anyone who tries to escape will be caught and given hard labour. Try again, and you will be placed in solitary confinement for a week.

Any further escape attempts will
be punished with THIS!' He pulled
a long feather from his belt and
waved it menacingly in the air.

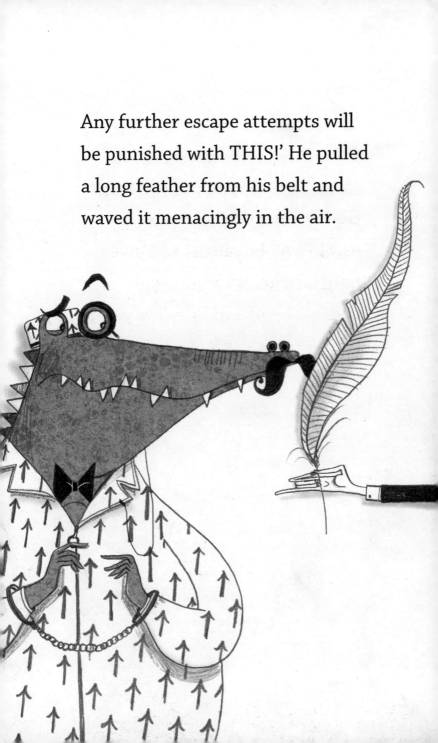

'You are here because you have committed terrible crimes,' he continued. 'I hope you will learn how to mend your ways and prepare for a new life of honesty and hard work.'

Foxy and Alphonso glanced at each other gloomily. 'Otherwise, prepare to be taken away by little old ladies who will make you roll over, beg and walk around the park – day in, day out, for the rest of your sad and sorry lives.'

And with that, Foxy DuBois, Alphonso Alligator and all the other prisoners were marched across the courtyard and up the steep stairs to their cells.

PSST...

41

Foxy and Alphonso
were arguing over whose
bed was whose when they
heard a quiet hiss. It was
coming from the next cell.

'Hey!' said the voice. 'You're
Foxy DuBois, ain't ya?'

'Who wants to know?' said Foxy,
suspiciously.

'I'm Eric-the-Evil,' said the voice.
'Busiest cab driver in Vaudeville
I was. Till I gets caught for
overcharging. Used to see ya, I did,
all them years ago. You in your fur
coat and high heels and all them
jewels... How comes you ended up
in a place like this?'

'I met the alligator of my dreams,' said Foxy. She reached between the bars and shook Eric's paw daintily. 'You don't happen to know how I might get out of this dump do you?'

'What? And risk the Feather of Doom?' said Eric-the-Evil. 'You'd be mad to try. Anyways, there ain't no escape from this hell hole. Believe me, if there was I'd be outta here like a rat out of a drainpipe.'

'Hmmm,' thought Foxy. 'We'll see about that.'

Chapter 3

In which Alphonso eats an apple pie and chokes on a bone. Eh??

After several days of hard thinking, Foxy had come up with a big, fat nothing. De nada. Zilch.

'You'd better think of something soon,' growled Alphonso.

'I'm so hungry, I could eat a...

PIE!!!'

Foxy snorted. 'Like THAT'S going
to happen,' she said gloomily.

But Alphonso wasn't listening because at that moment, a delicious smell was busy winding its way up his left nostril. It was coming from a trolley, stuffed with letters and parcels.

Pushing the trolley was a mangy grey cat who went by the name of Smokey Malone. He was such a fierce and notorious criminal, that the guards gave him special duties like delivering the mail and licking out the porridge bowl.

'Delivery for Mister Evil!' Smokey Malone thrust a large parcel towards Eric-the-Evil's cell. Quick as a flash, Alphonso reached through the bars and whipped it out of Smokey's hands. Then he

ripped open the paper and
sniffed dreamily. Inside was a
huge apple pie.

'I wouldn't eat that if I were you,'
mumbled Eric-the-Evil.

And if I were you, I wouldn't tell a hungry alligator what to do,' snapped Alphonso. He took an enormous bite and immediately fell to the floor, clutching his scaly throat. 'Gaaaarrggghhh!' he gasped.

'What now?' groaned Foxy, rolling her eyes.

'Got – a – bone!' gasped Alphonso, struggling for breath.

'Don't be stupid!' Foxy laughed. 'Apple pies don't have bones!'

'Just – get – it – out!' wheezed
the stricken alligator.

'What? Reach right down into
your jaws and pull out a non-
existent bone? I don't think so!'

But Alphonso begged and
pleaded and promised to give
Foxy anything if only she would
help him.

Foxy pondered for a long while.
Perhaps she could turn this to her
advantage. 'OK,' she said. 'I'll do it.
But in return you have to promise

to help me escape, and when we get out of here, you must pack your bags and leave. For good.'

Alphonso nodded vigorously. Foxy braced herself and reached right down into his slimy throat to pull out the bone. Only it wasn't a bone at all. It was a file. The sort a carpenter might use to smooth out splinters from a piece of wood.

Foxy's whiskers began to twitch and a sly smile spread across her foxy face.

'Planning a nice manicure were we, Eric?' she called. 'Isn't this nail file rather large for a scrawny little creature like you?'

Eric-the-Evil squirmed uncomfortably. 'I was gonna share it with you, 'onest,' he said.

'Course you were,' smiled Foxy. 'I'm sure Warden Gordon will be very impressed with your generosity.'

'Oh, please, Miss DuBois, don't

tell the warden! I'll do anything,'
Eric pleaded.

'Good,' said Foxy. 'You can start
by telling us how to use this
thing to escape.' She waved the
enormous file in the air, smiling
with satisfaction.

Chapter 4

In which Foxy attempts her first escape and ends up in a room full of pink frilly knickers

'I don't see why I have to do all the hard work,' growled Alphonso. 'I've been sawing away at these bars for hours!'

Foxy lifted her head from the book she was reading and surveyed Alphonso's handiwork. 'You're doing the work because I saved your life,' she yawned. 'And besides, I'm keeping watch.'

Suddenly there came a low whistle from Eric-the-Evil next door. The night guard was doing the rounds.

'Watch out!' hissed Foxy.

'Head count!'

Alphonso dived onto his bed and pretended to be asleep.

Foxy lay motionless, her eyes squeezed tightly shut as she

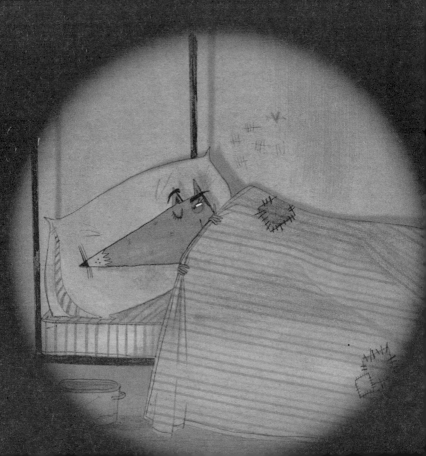

listened to the rustling feathers
of the night guard, stalking
along the corridor. She willed
him to pass them by, but he
stopped right outside and shone a
powerful torch into their cell.

Foxy was sure he'd see the broken
bars, but he did not sound the
alarm. He did not cry out, or
call for reinforcements. All Foxy
heard was a brief scuffle, a
strained gurgle, then nothing.

Breathing a sigh of relief, Foxy DuBois opened her eyes. She found Alphonso grinning dreamily. A single white feather drifted underneath his bed and lay lifeless in the dust. 'I don't know why you're looking so happy,' she snapped. 'We were nearly rumbled.'

Just before dawn the final bar came free. Foxy tied several bed sheets together to make a rope. It was barely strong enough to take the weight of a rather small fox, let alone the huge bulk of an over-fed alligator. But that suited Foxy just fine. The sooner she got rid of him, the better, even if he had promised to help her.

'When Alphonso climbs out of the window, the sheets will rip and he'll be a gonner for sure,' she thought.

All she had to do was persuade that dimwit to let her go first. She tied one end of the rope to her bed and threw the rest out of the window.

'This is it,' said Foxy innocently. 'Just a short climb down this lovely strong rope and we'll be out of here. After you,' she smiled.

Alphonso looked at the rope. Then he looked at Foxy. His yellow eyes narrowed. 'You're up to something,' he growled. 'I bet you've planned some scheming plan to get rid of me. Well I'm not that stupid. Oh no. You go first.'

'OK,' said Foxy quickly. She
grabbed the rope and was gone,
whooping with delight at her
clever trick.

'I'm free! I'm FREE! I'm – Oh!'

It was way past breakfast when
the guards finally managed to
winch Foxy to the ground. Then,
without a word, or even a cup of
tea, both Foxy and Alphonso were
marched into the work room for a
week of hard labour.

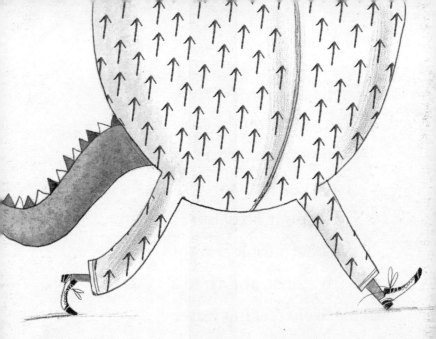

'This is your fault!' Alphonso snarled. 'I should eat you right now.'

'Suits me,' snapped Foxy. 'Then you can do my work as well as your own.'

'Why you double-crossing
mangy piece of fur!'
roared Alphonso.
He leapt at Foxy but
the guard took aim
with a hose and fired a
blast of freezing water
at them.

'Aaaarrggh!' yelled
Alphonso. 'That went
right down my ear!'

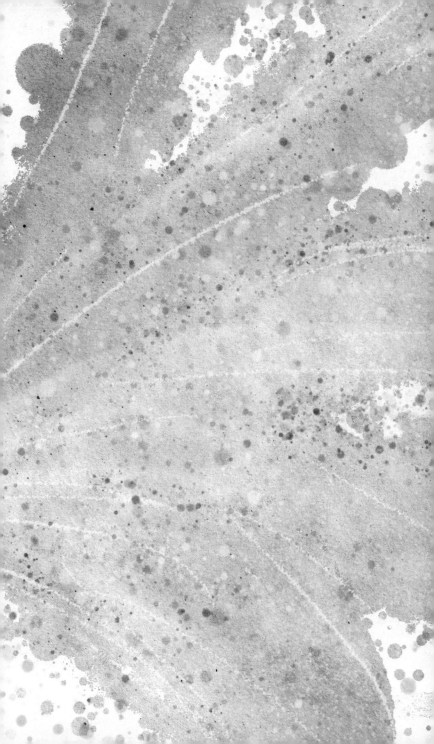

Foxy sat down soggily and sighed. 'Oh shut up and get on with your sewing,' she said.

Chapter 5

In which Foxy attempts her second escape and ends up with a very sore bottom

After making 2,651 pairs of frilly knickers, Foxy and Alphonso were finally returned to their cell.

'Ahhh!' grinned Alphonso, flopping onto his bed. 'Home, sweet home.'

Foxy just paced up and down restlessly. 'I've got to get out of here,' she moaned.

But Alphonso was not the least bit concerned. 'Hey, come on, Foxy,' he smiled. 'Relax a bit. Being in jail isn't all that bad.'

'What?' gaped Foxy. 'Being in jail is the most hideous, rotten thing in the world. It stinks for a start, the food is terrible and have you seen the looks I get from that creep Smokey Malone?'

Alphonso licked his lips and gazed down the corridor as if waiting for something. But it was only the guard, doing his rounds.

'Oh, I think the food is quite good,' he drooled. 'As for the other prisoners – they are always very polite to me.' He picked his razor sharp teeth with a powerful claw and smiled, contentedly. 'Plus, I get to laze around all day and annoy you. What more could an alligator want?'

***

As the days dragged by, Foxy DuBois grew thinner and thinner on the meagre diet of watery grey slop and stale bread.

Strangely, Alphonso did not seem to be losing weight at all. In fact, he was looking positively plump.

One hot day, as they were melting in their cell, Foxy said, 'I just don't understand it. I'm eating everything they give me and getting thinner and thinner. You're eating practically nothing and getting fatter and fatter. How can that be?'

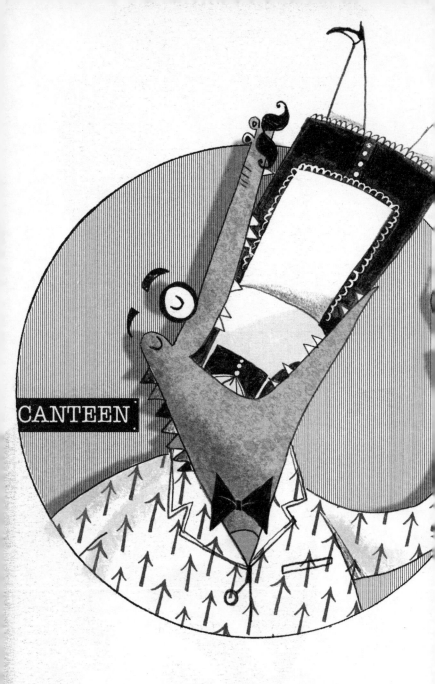

CANTEEN

Alphonso looked away, blushing, as he plucked a white feather from between his teeth. 'Oh, I just look at food and it goes straight onto my hips,' he sighed dreamily.

Alphonso's daydream was rudely interrupted by the voice of a new guard strutting past.

'Volunteers wanted to tidy up Warden Gordon's garden!' he shouted.

'Ooh, me please,' said Alphonso, sarcastically. 'A whole day slaving away in the baking hot sun would be so much nicer than relaxing here. Not.'

But, much to Alphonso's disgust, Foxy DuBois jumped to her feet and called out through the bars. 'Oh, please, Mister Guard, my friends and I would LOVE to lend a hand. We're expert gardeners.'

And so it was that Foxy, Alphonso and Eric-the-Evil were taken into the yard and put to work.

Alphonso kicked at the dust
and sulked about working on an
empty stomach. Meanwhile, Foxy
and Eric-the-Evil pulled up weeds
from Warden Gordon's cabbage
patch, and watered his tomatoes.

'You'd better 'ave a good reason
for draggin' me outta me cell,
Miss DuBois,' hissed Eric-the-Evil.

'Oh, but I have,' grinned Foxy.
'And if you want to get away from
here as much as I do, you'll help
me. Just fetch that wheelbarrow.'

Foxy dug up a huge, wriggling
worm and when Eric-the-Evil
returned, she dropped it down
Alphonso's back.

The surprised reptile let
out a blood curdling roar.
He started rolling around
in the dust, trying to stop
the unbearable tickling.

While the guards were busy calming him down, Foxy crept over to Warden Gordon's scarecrow and quickly pinched his ragged old guard clothes. Then she ordered Eric-the-Evil to put them on. Foxy climbed into the wheelbarrow and told Eric-the-Evil to cover her with weeds and old cabbage leaves. 'Now wheel me out of the gate,' she hissed.

Eric-the-Evil pulled up the scarecrow's collar and pulled down the scarecrow's hat, so his tiny snout was only just showing.

He pushed the wheelbarrow
casually towards the gates.

'Hey there!' called one of the
guards. 'Where are you going
with that barrow?'

'Special orders from his Gordon-ness,' barked Eric-the-Evil in his biggest voice, which was not very big. 'Got to depositate these weeds outside the gates on the double.'

'Right you are,' said the guard. He was just waving Eric-the-Evil through when a strange sound came from beneath the weeds.

AAAA...

AAAA...

AAAA-AAAA-A

AAAA-

A-ATCHOO!

'Looks like you might have a little stowaway in there!' the guard said. 'Can't have you getting in a tangle with a rat or anything.' He picked up a garden fork and drove it into the weeds.

100

Foxy burst out from
the rotting vegetation,
clutching her bottom
and howling.

The guard turned to
Eric-the-Evil and whipped
the scarecrow's hat from
his head. 'Nice try, Mister
Evil,' he chuckled. Then he
marched the two scoundrels
back inside, shoved them into
solitary confinement
and locked the door.

Chapter 6

In which Alphonso's plan is more fool-ISH than fool-PROOF

After a long, lonely week locked in the cupboard under the stairs, Eric-the-Evil and Foxy DuBois returned to their cells.

'Told you there was no way outta here,' grumbled Eric-the-Evil.

Foxy was so weak from lack
of food and sunlight that she
just lay on her bed, pulled the
scratchy blanket up to her ears,
and groaned.

Alphonso, on the other hand, was as fat and happy as Foxy was thin and miserable.

'Hey, cheer up, Foxy,' he grinned. 'Today is your lucky day.'

'Oh yeah? And how did you work that out?'

'Because,' beamed Alphonso, 'today is the day you get to watch me walk out of here to freedom.'

'Yeah, right!' laughed Foxy.
'What are you going to do?
Eat your way out?'

Alphonso considered the suggestion for a while, then shook his head. 'Actually, I've got a much better plan. A foolproof plan that I've been saving for the right moment.'

That ridiculous rancid reptile had a plan? This was incredible! Foxy threw her arms around the alligator's enormous belly. 'I'll buy you the biggest pig-out you've ever had, just please, please tell me your plan!' she gushed. 'What are we going to do?'

With a superior smile and a confident swagger, Alphonso dug into his pocket and produced a crumpled, yellowed card. 'I don't know what you are going to do,' he said, 'but I'm going to use THIS.'

Eric-the-Evil burst out laughing. 'Oh, Foxy! That crocodile of yours really is priceless!'

Foxy slumped on her bunk and put her head in her paws. 'Oh my days,' she groaned.

When Eric-the-Evil explained the Get Out of Jail Free card was from a game, Alphonso had an almighty tantrum! He gnawed at the thick steel bars with his sharp teeth and jumped up and down on the hard concrete floor.

STAMP!

'Get me out of here!' sobbed Alphonso. He lunged at Foxy, grabbing pleadingly at her overalls. Foxy dodged to the side, desperate to avoid the clinging, wailing reptile and the pair ran round and round their cell in a frenzy. Suddenly Alphonso skidded into the wall and let out a terrible yelp of pain.

'Ow ow ow ow owwwwwww!' he wailed.

His claw had got caught in a
metal grille and ripped it off
the wall. It hurt like crazy.
Foxy stopped in her tracks
and gaped in awe at
the damage.

'Well, well, well,' she smiled.
'Just look at that.'

In the wall, where the grille had once been, was a hole. Not a big hole, but a hole nonetheless.

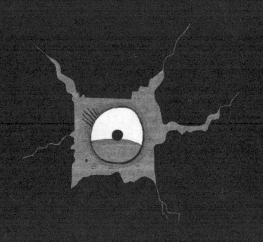

As she stuck her snout into the dark void, a slight breeze tickled Foxy's whiskers and a sly smile spread across her foxy face. 'If the air can get in,' she mused, 'then I can get out!' She picked at the edge of the hole with her claw, scraping away the crumbling concrete. By the time Alphonso had stopped wailing, she had a large pile of dust and rubble by her feet.

'Alphonso,' she hissed. 'Stop fussing and make yourself useful!'

Soon the hole was big enough for Foxy to squeeze through, but there was a problem. It was nearly exercise time and they could hear a guard approaching. Quick as a flash, Foxy shoved Alphonso in front of the hole, grabbed a pack of cards and pretended to play.

'Exercise time. Get a move on.'

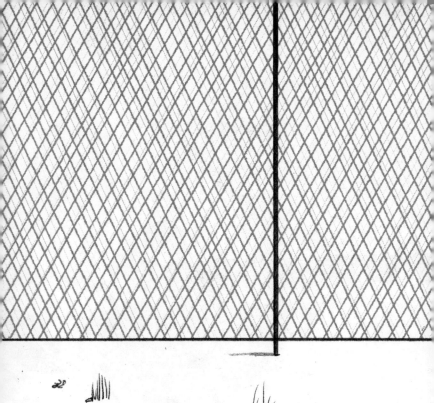

'Just a couple more days of
digging and the hole will be big
enough for you to get through
too,' said Foxy as she and
Alphonso walked around the yard.
'Then we'll be as free as birds.'

But Foxy had no intention of
waiting more than a few hours,
let alone a few days. She was
getting out tonight. If Alphonso
was too fat to escape with her,
so much the better.

Chapter 7

In which Foxy is caught between a rock and a hard place. Or, rather, between a giant warty backside and death by sewage.

T hat evening, on the stroke of midnight, while Alphonso was slumped in his bed, no doubt dreaming of chicken pie, Foxy DuBois gathered up her few possessions.

She quickly padded across the cell and slipped into the hole.

The ventilation tunnel was narrow and slippery. Foxy followed her nose until she reached a large fan which brought fresh air in from outside. She peered through the rotating blades to see the prison yard below and the fields and trees beyond.

'So far, so good,' thought Foxy.
She loosened the rusty screws
on another metal grille and
squeezed out of the tunnel into
a small, dark room.

Set into the floor in front of her
was a wooden trap door. But
when she lifted it open, Foxy
was almost knocked out by
the most horrendous, stench.
'Ewwwww!' she cried. 'Sewage!'

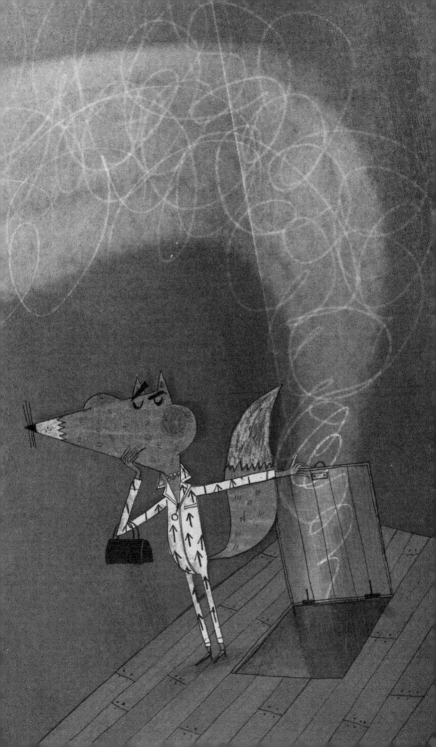

Now, any sensible prison
escapee would have plunged into
the sewage pipe and followed
it in a downhill direction. After
all, it was bound to end up
somewhere outside the prison
grounds. But not
Foxy DuBois. Oh no.

'I may be a
criminal,' she thought,
'but I am still a lady,
and there is no way on
this earth that I am going to
set even one toe inside a pipe
filled with other people's – '

ELLLPPP!'

Foxy whipped around to see
a large, green warty backside
sticking out of the opening in the
ventilation tunnel.

It was Alphonso.
Or, rather, it was
Alphonso's behind.
The rest of him was still
inside the ventilation
shaft. 'What an idiot!'
Foxy groaned.

And then she groaned some
more. With Alphonso wedged
in the ventilation shaft, and
the only way out through a pipe
full of sewage, Foxy DuBois was
stuck too!

Try as she might, Foxy could
not prize Alphonso free.
'It's no good,' she wheezed.
'You're too fat!'

'Well, I may have been eating a
few extra snacks lately,' mumbled
Alphonso's behind.

'A few extra snacks?'

'Only the odd guard or two,' said Alphonso defensively. 'An alligator's got to eat! And anyway, I hid their uniforms under my bunk, so nobody will know.'

Foxy's whiskers began to twitch and a sly smile spread across her foxy face. 'Exactly how many guards did you eat? One? Two? Five?' she asked hopefully.

'What?!'

'I didn't eat them all at once!'
growled Alphonso. 'I saved the last
two for this morning's breakfast,
and now I'm going to be stuck in
this stupid tunnel for ever, thanks
to you!'

Foxy began to chuckle. Then
she roared with laughter. 'Oh,
Alphonso!' she gasped. 'You really
are the most useless predator I
have ever met!'

HA! HA! HA!
A! ha! HA! HA! HA! HA! HA!
HA! HA! HA! HA! ha! HA! HA! ha!
A- ha! HA! HA! ha! HA! ha!
ha! HA! HA! HA! ha! HA! HA!
HA! ha! HA! HA! HA! HA! HA! ha!
HA! ha! HA! HA! HA!

Two days later, after Alphonso had starved enough for Foxy to heave him back into the ventilation tunnel, the two rogues crawled back up to their cell.

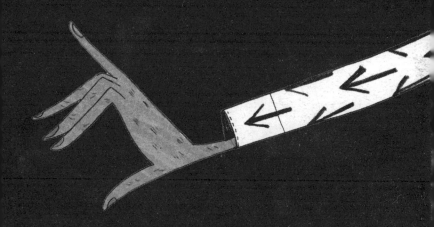

Straightaway, Foxy dived
underneath Alphonso's bunk
and retrieved several sets of
keys from the unfortunate
guards' uniforms.

She wished she could think of a way to leave Alphonso locked up inside, but all was not lost. He had promised to pack his bags and leave once they escaped. With a grin on her face she unlocked the door, then tossed the keys to Eric-the-Evil. The three of them strolled out of the jail, as free as birds.

Chapter 8

In which Foxy and Alphonso end up right back where they started

'Hey, Blue-eyes! You're back!' Tony Ravioli rushed up to Foxy and gave her a hug. 'Did they let you out early for good behaviour?'

'Something like that,' said Foxy.
'Meet Eric-the – errr, Eric-the-
Taxi-Driver.'

Tony took Eric-the-Evil's paw
and pumped it up and down.
'Pleasure to meet you, Mister
Driver,' he beamed.

Foxy ordered burgers
and chips for everyone
and they all tucked
in, hungrily.

'And now, my dear reptilian
friend,' she said, nudging
Alphonso, 'it's time for you to
keep your promise.'

Alphonso looked up, mid-guzzle.
'What promise?' he asked. 'I
don't remember any promise.'

'Yes you do,' insisted Foxy.
'The one where I agreed to place
myself in mortal danger to
remove that painful object
from your throat and you
promised to pack your bags
and leave for ever.'

Alphonso thought for a while.
'Oh, that promise,' he said. 'Well,
actually, I've changed my mind.'

'You... you can't do that!'
Foxy spluttered. 'We had an
agreement!!'

But Alphonso just grinned
wickedly. 'Well, you know that old
saying: "Never trust an alligator.
Especially one with a nail file
stuck in his throat." You're lucky
to be alive, Foxy DuBois. Perhaps
I should have just eaten you there
and then, while I had the chance.

Perhaps I'll just eat you now, instead.' He rose from his seat and moved towards her.

'Oh, there's no need for that,' said Foxy, hurriedly. 'I was just kidding. I don't really want you to move out. I'd miss you.'

'Awww, really?' Alphonso sniffed.

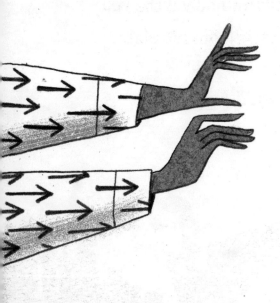

'Err – no.' Foxy dived for cover, narrowly avoiding Alphonso's claws and the naughty pair chased each other out of the East Street Eazy Diner and off down the road. Eric-the-Evil shook his head, smiled and licked the last greasy morsels from his plate. Life was good.

The End

ALPHONSO'S GET OUT OF JAIL APPLE PIE

FOR THE PASTRY

500g plain flour
100g icing sugar, sifted
250g butter cut into small cubes
Zest of 1 lemon
2 large eggs
1 splash of milk

FOR THE FILLING

6 large bramley apples
(cooking apples)
50g butter
100g caster sugar
half a tsp cinnamon
1 egg, beaten

EITHER: 1 stick of super-charged dynamite, OR: 150g of blackberries
26cm pie dish, buttered / Oven 180ºC / 350ºF / Gas 4

FIRST MAKE YOUR PASTRY DOUGH

1. Sieve the flour and icing sugar into a large bowl.
2. Chuck in the cut up butter and rub into the flour.
3. Add lemon zest, eggs and milk.
4. Squidge it all together until you have a ball.
5. Wrap the dough in cling film and put it in the fridge for half an hour to get it nice and cold.

NEXT MAKE THE APPLE FILLING

1. Peel the apples.
2. Cut them into 8 wedges and scoop out the cores.

3. Put the butter and sugar in a large pan and melt them together.

4. Add the apples and cook slowly for 15 minutes with the lid ON.

5. Add the dynamite or blackberries and cook for another 5 minutes with the lid OFF.

6. Add the cinnamon.

THEN ROLL OUT YOUR PASTRY

1. Cut your pastry in half.

2. Roll out each half to about 29cm wide using a rolling pin.

3. Place one disc of pastry into the pie dish and press down gently.

ASSEMBLE YOUR PIE

1. Slop the filling on top, then place the other round piece of pastry on top of the filling and press down gently.

2. Paint some egg on the edges and crimp them together so they stick.

3. Paint the top of your pie with beaten egg and sprinkle with some sugar.

4. Place the whole thing on a baking tray at the bottom of the oven. Cook for 50-60 minutes.

5. Slice and serve with custard, cream or ice cream – or all three if you are an alligator. Yum!

HOW TO SURVIVE JAIL IN 5 EASY STEPS
By Alphonso Alligator

1. Keep yourself entertained by annoying your cellmate. Choose from the following irritating activities:

- humming incessantly
- trumping
- snoring
- burping
- asking: 'Can we go home now?' fifty thousand times a day

2. Do some knitting. If you don't have proper wool, make your own by unravelling your cellmate's pyjamas.

3 . Keep cool. Ask your cellmate to fan you with a large newspaper. If they refuse, threaten to eat them.

4 . Learn origami. If you don't have any proper paper, simply tear the pages out of your cellmate's book.

5 . Eat everything and anything, including your cellmate's dinner. They will thank you for it one day.*

*They will never thank you for anything, but that's life.

Every Fox's Essential Kit For Jail

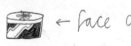 ← face cream

earplugs

nail varnish

perfume

clothes peg

mascara

whisker wax

4.
to
wax,

5. Pict
to stick
you of th

1. Earplugs – to block out snoring, humming, screaming, groaning and other annoying noises.

2. Clothes peg – for blocking out horrendous smells such as alligator trumps.

    ...alad cream – to hide the ... of revolting prison food.

    ...ck, mascara, curling ...e cream, nail varnish ...me.

    ...Ebenezer Jones ... wall to remind ...times.

ALPHONSO'S GET-OUT-OF-EVERYTHING-FREE CARDS

You never know when you might find yourself stuck in a tricky place, so here are some free Get Out cards, should you ever need them.

Photocopy this page then cut out the cards and keep them with you at all times.

GET OUT OF JAIL FREE

GET OUT OF
TIDYING YOUR
ROOM FREE

GET OUT OF
HOMEWORK
FREE

NB: Each card may be used only once.

GET OUT OF
WRITING THANK YOU
CARDS FREE

GET OUT OF
WATCHING THE
BABY FREE

GET OUT OF WALKING THE DOG FREE

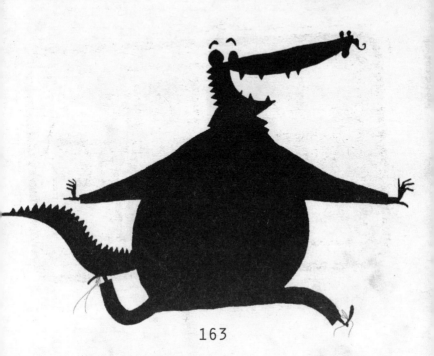

163

An Interview with Warden Gordon

By

ANN RICE-PUDDING

Ann: Working in a jail must be a difficult job. Do you enjoy it?

Warden Gordon: Oh yes! I love making the inmates suffer.

Ann: What were you like as a child?

Warden Gordon: I was very happy. I spent most of my time teasing and taunting other children and being cruel to small animals.

Ann: Err... right. How nice. Tell me, who do you most admire in the world?

Warden Gordon: Who do I most admire? ME! Of course. Don't you?

Ann: Umm, well, I...

Warden Gordon: How about I take you out for dinner? I know a nice cheap place on East Street.

Ann: I really don't think...

Warden Gordon: I'll make it worth your while...

Ann: NO!! Err... I mean, no. Thank you. I'm pretty sure I'm busy. Yes. I am. Very. Busy.

Warden Gordon: Hrmph. Suit yourself. But you'll never get this chance again.

Ann: I think I can live with that. Just.

Foxy's Favourite places

White Sandy Bay
Good for lazing about in the sun drinking pink lemonade.

Ms Markos's Shoe Emporium
They have all the latest styles.

The Ritz Movie House
Great for escaping from the humdrum of daily life. And for swooning over Ebenezer Jones, my favourite film star.

Shelfridges
They have dresses to die for.

Frotescue & Matrons
For the finer things in life.

Mr BILLY BONGO
Exclusive

Mr Billy Bongo loves:

* Having his ears combed.
* Stealing socks.
* Hiding in small places then jumping out to scare people.
* Barking at cats, as long as they are OUTSIDE and he is INSIDE.

Mr Billy Bongo hates:

* Going out in the rain.
* Wearing nail varnish.
* Cats, especially when they are OUTSIDE and he is is INSIDE.
* Dog food. Sushi is SO much nicer.

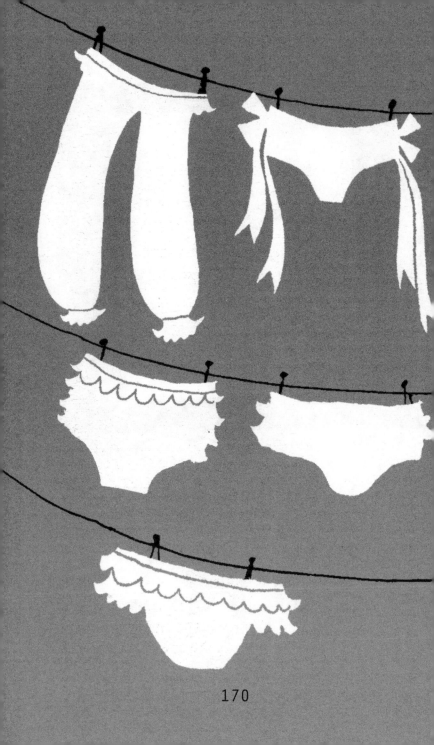

Frilly Knicker Designs

Here's some of the frilly knickers that Foxy and Alphonso made. Photocopy this page then add your own snazzy designs.

JAILBREAK GAME

★ Split into two teams: the seeking team and the hiding team.

★ Choose a spot for the 'jail' such as the stairs.

★ The seeking team counts 1-50 whilst the other team hides.

★ When they have finished counting, the seeking team searches for the hiding players.

★ When caught, the hiding players must go to 'jail'.

★ The only way to get out jail is to be 'jail broken'. In order to be 'jail broken', a player from the hiding team that has not been sent to jail can touch the jail and shout 'jail break' and everyone is freed.

★ The game ends when every player on the hiding team is caught and then the players switch sides.

What are Foxy and Alphonso arguing about his time!?
You decide!

Photocopy this page then add your own speech.